DREAMWORKS

GABBY'S DOLLHOUSE

MER-MAZING ADVENTURE

Adapted by
Gabrielle Reyes

SCHOLASTIC INC.

It's time to unbox a **DOLLHOUSE DELIVERY**!

Inside the Kitty Cat Surprise Box is a little bottle with a mermaid inside.

"Wait a minute . . . This is MerCat's sister, SunnyCat!"

I shake the bottle, and SunnyCat comes to life!

"Sparkling sea creatures!" SunnyCat says. "Today is the **MERMAID SPARKLE PARTY** in Mermaid-Lantis. You've just got to come! Go see MerCat. She knows the way!"

Before long, we're all aboard the SS *MerCat*!

"Check out our mermaid tails!" I say to Pandy Paws.

"Whoa!" Pandy Paws says. "Paw-some!"

"You only need three things to come to the Mermaid Sparkle Party in Mermaid-Lantis," SunnyCat says.

"Your FIN . . ."

"Your GRIN . . ."

"And your SPARKLE within!"

"Where do we find our sparkle?" asks Pandy Paws.

"Your sparkle is that special thing that makes you happy," says MerCat.

"Hmm . . . ," I say. "Singing my song that helps me shrink down always makes me happy." I sing and pinch my cat ears.

I look down, and wow! "Hey, I found my sparkle!"

Hug attacks always make Pandy Paws happy.

He gives MerCat a big hug—and finds his sparkle, too!

We dive off the ship and into the blue water.

Swish, swish go our mermaid tails.

Soon we arrive at MERMAID-LANTIS!

"This place is mer-mazing!" I say.

"Would you like a tour?" SunnyCat asks. "We can take the Rainbow Slide!"

MerCat and SunnyCat put in three crystals, and . . .

. . . the **RAINBOW SLIDE** appears!

"Let's slide!" MerCat says.

And off we go!

The slide goes all around Mermaid-Lantis.

There's **MAGIC** everywhere!

We pass some mini mermaids. "Aw! Have you ever seen anything as cute as this?"

A spa!

"Look at that cat-tabulous hair!"

"These homemade mermaid cakes
are tasty-licious!"

"This place is mer-tastic!" I say.

At the bottom of the slide, we land on a big stage shaped like a clamshell.

"This is the MERMAID SPARKLE STAGE!" says SunnyCat. "Here, everyone will share the special thing that makes them happy."

"I can't wait to see everyone's sparkle!" I say.

But not everyone in Mermaid-Lantis is excited for the party.

Over in a corner of the stage, Kitty Squiddy sulks.

"*Sparkle schmarkle*. Everyone has their special sparkle except me," he mutters. "I wish there was a way to stop this Sparkle Party."

Suddenly, Kitty Squiddy has an idea.

"If I take the crystals from the bottom of the Rainbow Slide, the slide will disappear. No slide, no Sparkle Party!"

Kitty Squiddy zips over. He grabs the crystals.

Swipe, swipe, swipe.

I turn around just in time to see him swim away before the Rainbow Slide disappears!

"Sinking seaweed! Kitty Squiddy swiped our crystals," MerCat says.

With no Rainbow Slide, other guests won't be able to get to the party.

"The Sparkle Party's canceled?" Pandy Paws asks.

"It's not canceled *yet*," I say. "We can go talk to Kitty Squiddy."

SunnyCat leads us to Kitty Squiddy's cave.

"There must be a reason Kitty Squiddy took the crystals," I say as we hide behind a rock. "Let's see if we can figure it out."

Inside the cave, Kitty Squiddy doesn't notice us. He's singing a special song and dancing.

"Kitty Squiddy sure loves to dance," Pandy Paws whispers. "Look at all his moves."

Kitty Squiddy
stretches his arms
HIGH.

He squiggles **LOW**.

Kitty Squiddy
lands in a **SPLIT**!

"Moves or no moves," SunnyCat says, leading us inside, "he needs to give back those crystals!"

Kitty Squiddy whirls around. "Nope! No Sparkle Party for *me*. No Sparkle Party for *anyone*!"

"But don't you want to show your special sparkle?" asks Pandy Paws. "And see everyone else's, too?"

Kitty Squiddy frowns. "I don't have a special sparkle."

"Sure you do," says Pandy Paws. "What do you do that makes you feel happy?"

"You mean, like dancing?" Kitty Squiddy twirls around.

"That's it!" I say.

Kitty Squiddy begins to glow.

"You've found your sparkle!" MerCat says.

"SKOODLE-Y DOODLE-Y DEE!" says Kitty Squiddy. "A special sparkle for *me*!"

Kitty Squiddy stops dancing.

"I'm sorry for taking the crystals. I can help you put them back."

We swim back to the Sparkle Stage and put the crystals back where they belong.

"Rainbow Slide activated!" SunnyCat says.

Kitty Squiddy stretches his arms up high as we slide back to the Sparkle Stage.

"SKOODLE-Y DOODLE-Y DEE! It's time for the Sparkle Party!" he shouts.

"You have your sparkle within," I tell Kitty Squiddy. "You have your happy grin. Now all you need is your mermaid fin!"

I have an idea. "Since you need your whole body to dance, your special sparkly fin can be a special sparkly HAT!"

Kitty Squiddy puts on his mermaid fin hat.
He stretches high and squiggles low.
"SKOODLE-Y DOODLE-Y DOO! Now I'm sparkly, too!"

Kitty Squiddy found his special sparkle!
WHAT'S YOURS?